For Ella — KU
For all my nephews and nieces — AC

The Sophie Rabbit Books:
Sophie and Abigail
Sophie and the wonderful picture
Sophie and the Mother's Day card
Sophie in charge

This edition published in the UK 2004 by
Mathew Price Limited
The Old Glove Factory, Bristol Road
Sherborne, Dorset DT9 4HP
Text copyright © Kaye Umansky 1995
Illustrations copyright © Anna Currey 1995
Edited by Belinda Hollyer
The right of Kaye Umansky and Anna Currey
to be identified as authors of this work
has been asserted by them in accordance with
the Copyright, Designs and Patents Act, 1988
All rights reserved

ISBN 1-84248-109-6

Printed in China

Kaye Umansky

Sophie and the wonderful picture

Illustrated by *Anna Currey*

MATHEW PRICE LIMITED

Sophie Rabbit and Graham Frog
had painted a wonderful picture.

It had taken them all morning,
and they had used up nearly all
the green paint, but Mrs Badger said
it was worth it.

"Look, everyone!" cried Mrs Badger when she saw it. "Just stop for a moment, and look at this lovely painting. What is it, you two?"

"It's the pond where I live," explained Graham. "That's my lily pad there, look. And those green blobs are all my relations. Sophie painted those. Go on Sophie, tell them."

Sophie blushed and shook her head.

"You do it, Graham," she whispered. "You're so much better at explaining things than me."

So Graham explained all about the painting. He did it so well that when he finished, the class clapped.

"Tomorrow, your mums and dads will be coming to see the end of term assembly," said Mrs Badger. "Would you like to show your painting?"

"Yes please," said Graham immediately.

But Sophie wasn't so sure.

"I'm scared of standing up in front of everyone," she confided to Graham. "I'll feel shy. All those eyes staring at me!"

"Don't worry," said Graham. "I'll do all the talking. All you have to do is hold it the right way up."

"Are you coming to assembly tomorrow?" Sophie asked her mum and dad, when she got home.

"Of course, love," said her mum.

"Wild ferrets wouldn't keep me away," said Sophie's dad. "Especially now I know our Soph's the star."

"I'm not doing much," said Sophie. "Just holding up a painting. Graham's doing all the talking. My bit's not at all important."

But that night, Sophie couldn't get
to sleep.

"What's up, Soph?" asked her dad
when he came to tuck her in. "Is it
stage fright?"

Sophie nodded.

"Suppose I hold it upside down?"
she whispered. "What if I drop it?"

"You won't," said George Rabbit.
"But if you do, just keep smiling.
You can get away with most things if
you've got a big smile on your face."

The following morning, the school hall
was crammed with everyone's relations.

Sophie's mum and dad arrived early,
and sat near the door so that Gareth
could be taken out if he played up.
Sophie's dad gave her a big wink, and
Sophie gave him a timid little wave.

As for Graham's relations – well!
They took up the whole front row
looking proud enough to burst.

"Good morning, everyone," said
Mrs Badger. "To start our show,
Gordon Fox, Andrew Otter and
Rebecca Water-Rat will do a dance
entitled *Falling Leaves*."

Gordon, Andrew and Rebecca stood up,
Mrs Badger took her place at
the piano, and the show began.

The Falling Leaves danced
beautifully, and got a big clap.

So did Kelly and Fran Mouse,
when they sang their cheese song.

Terry Tortoise showed a fishing rod
he had made, and everyone nodded
and said how clever he was.

Then it was Graham and Sophie's turn.

"Graham and Sophie will now tell you all about their new picture," said Mrs Badger.

Sophie's mum and dad craned their necks.

Graham's relations sat up straight, and nudged each other excitedly.

"Stand up, you two. Hold it up high, Sophie, so everyone can see," said Mrs Badger.

Heart in her mouth, Sophie stood up
and held the picture high.

"Come on Graham," she whispered.
"Stand up! It's our turn."

But Graham didn't move.

To everyone's surprise, he just sat there.

His face looked a paler green than usual.

He stared miserably at all his expectant relations. He opened his mouth, but no sound came out.

Desperately, he rolled his eyes
at Sophie, and shook his head.

"Can't!" he said, in a small,
strangled voice.

It was true. Graham couldn't.

"All right," whispered Sophie. "You do the holding. I'll do the talking."

Gratefully, Graham stood up, took the picture, and held it high.

Sophie caught George Rabbit's eye. She took a deep breath, gave a wobbly smile, and began to speak.

"This is a painting we did of Graham's pond," she said, in a clear voice. "This is Graham's lily pad, and this is a mayfly, and these are reeds.

And these are all his relations ..."

And Sophie told the audience all about the painting, while Graham held it as high as he possibly could.

When she had finished, there came
a storm of applause.

Graham's relations stood up
and cheered, and so did Sophie's
mum and dad. Even Gareth joined in.

"Thanks, Sophie. I'm sorry about
that," whispered Graham. "It was
all those eyes, staring at me!"

"I know what you mean," said Sophie,
waving at her mum and dad, who were
still clapping their paws off.

"You were really good," said Graham.
"I thought you said you were shy?"

"I was," said Sophie, her eyes
shining. "Once. But not any more."